Crystal the Snow Fairy

For my friend, Joe Heaney,

who has always been

magical to me!

Special thanks to

Narinder Dhami

ISBN-13: 978-0-439-81387-7
ISBN-10: 0-439-81387-5

24 23 15/0

Printed in the U.S.A.

Crystal the Snow Fairy

by Daisy Meadows

SCHOLASTIC INC.
New York Toronto London Auckland Sydney
Mexico City New Delhi Hong Kong Buenos Aires

The Fairyland Palace
Forest of
Candy Factory
The Village Hall
River
Wetherbury Village

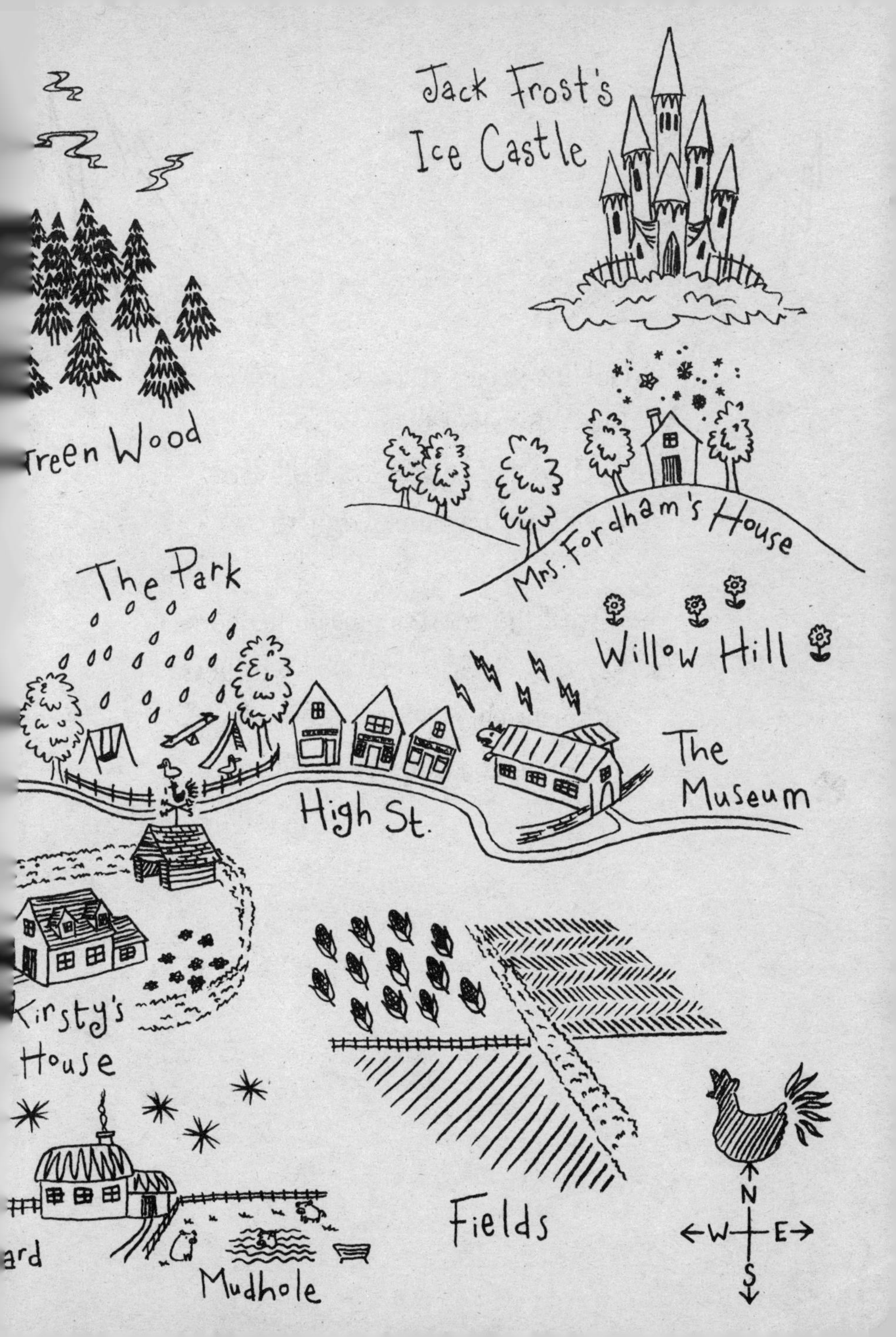

Jack Frost's
Ice Castle
Wood
Mrs. Fordham's House
The Park
Willow Hill
The
Museum
High St.
Kirsty's
House
Fields
Mudhole
N
W
E
S

Goblins green and goblins small,
I cast this spell to make you tall.
As high as the palace you shall grow.
My icy magic makes it so.

Then steal the rooster's magic feathers,
used by the fairies to make all weathers.
Climate chaos I have planned
on Earth, and here, in Fairyland!

Contents

A Magical Surprise

"Isn't it a beautiful day, Mom?" Kirsty Tate asked happily. She gazed out of the car window at the blue sky and sunshine. "Do you think it will stay like this for all of summer vacation?"

Mrs. Tate laughed. "Well, let's hope so," she said. "But remember what the weather

was like on Rainspell Island? It was always changing!"

Kirsty smiled to herself. She and her parents had been to Rainspell Island for vacation during the last school break. Kirsty had made a new friend there, Rachel Walker, and the two girls now shared a very special secret. They were friends with the fairies! When evil Jack Frost had put a spell on the seven Rainbow Fairies and banished them from Fairyland, Rachel and Kirsty had helped the fairy sisters get back home.

"Could Rachel come and stay with us for a little while, Mom? Please?" Kirsty asked, as they pulled up outside their house. The Tates lived in Wetherbury, a pretty village in the middle of the countryside.

"That's a really good idea," Mrs. Tate agreed. "Now, let's take this stuff inside."

"OK," said Kirsty, climbing out of the car. "Where's Dad?"

Just then, a voice called out from the distance. "Hello, I'm up here!"

Kirsty glanced up, shading her eyes against the sun. To the left of the house was an old wooden barn. Mr. Tate was standing at the top of a ladder next to the barn, holding a hammer.

"I'm just repairing the barn roof," he explained. "It's been leaking."

"Oh, dear," said Mrs. Tate, opening the car trunk. She handed two shopping bags to Kirsty. "We really have to do something about that barn. It's falling down."

"I like it," Kirsty replied. Suddenly, she jumped. Something cold and wet had landed on her nose! "Oh, no!" she exclaimed. "I think it's raining." Then she stared at the white flakes that had landed on her pink shirt. "It's not rain," she gasped. "It's *snow*!"

"Snow?" Mrs. Tate looked shocked. "In summer? It can't be!"

But it *was* snowing. In a flash, the sky had turned gray and snowflakes were floating down.

"Quick, Kirsty, let's get inside!" called Mrs. Tate, grabbing the rest of the shopping bags and closing the trunk of the car.

Mr. Tate was already climbing down from the ladder. They all rushed inside as the snow swirled around them.

"This is very strange," said Mr. Tate, frowning. "I wonder how long it will last?"

Kirsty glanced out of the kitchen window. "Mom, Dad, the snow stopped already!" she cried.

Mr. and Mrs. Tate joined Kirsty at the window. The sun was shining and the sky was blue. A few puddles of water were all that remained of the sudden snowstorm.

"Well!" said Mr. Tate. "How strange! It was almost like magic!"

Kirsty's heart began to pound. Could there be magic in the air? But why? She and Rachel had found all of the Rainbow Fairies, and Jack Frost had promised not to harm them again. Everything was fine in Fairyland now, wasn't it?

"You'd better go and change out of that wet shirt, Kirsty," said her mom.

Kirsty turned away from the window.

As she did, she spotted something on the kitchen table. It was a rusty old metal weather vane in the shape of a rooster. "What's that?" she asked.

"I found it in the park this morning," her father said. "It will look great on top of the barn once I'm done fixing the roof."

Kirsty reached a hand toward the weather vane. As she did, the metal glowed, and glittering sparkles danced toward her fingers. Kirsty blinked in surprise. When she looked again, the sparkles had vanished. All she could see was the rusty metal.

Confused, Kirsty ran upstairs to change. Had she imagined the sparkles? Maybe. The snow was real, though. She was sure of that. "I'll call Rachel after lunch," she thought. "Maybe she's been noticing strange things, too."

Kirsty hurried into her bedroom. There, on a shelf above her bed, was the snow globe the fairies had given her. It was a very special thank-you gift for helping the Rainbow Fairies. Rachel had one, too. It was filled with glittering fairy dust, in all the colors of the rainbow. When the snow globe was shaken up, the dust swirled and sparkled inside.

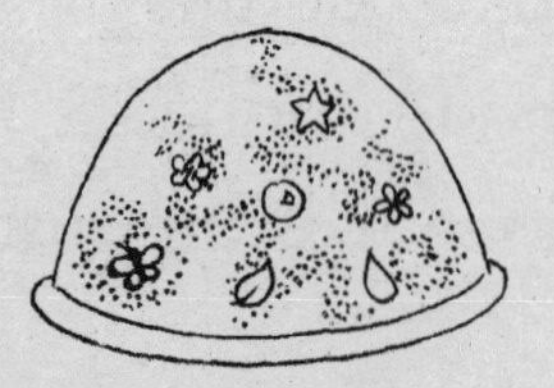

Right now, no one was shaking the snow globe — but the fairy dust was swirling around inside the glass! Kirsty forgot about her wet shirt and kept staring at the sparkling snow globe. She couldn't believe her eyes. "It must be magic!" she whispered.

She ran across the room and grabbed the glass globe, but then dropped it with a gasp of pain. The snow globe was so hot it had burned her fingers!

As the globe fell, it hit the edge of the shelf and shattered.

"Oh no!" Kirsty exclaimed, upset

that she'd broken her beautiful gift. Just then, sparkling fairy dust flew into the air, and floated down around her. Before she knew it, Kirsty was shrinking! It was just like on Rainspell Island. She and Rachel had become fairy-size when they helped rescue the Rainbow Fairies. Now she was tiny all over again!

Kirsty twisted around to look over her shoulder. There were her fairy wings, delicate and glittering. "Maybe the fairies want me to fly to Fairyland to see them," Kirsty said to herself. "But I don't know how to get there!"

As she spoke, the fairy dust drifted around her. Suddenly, a strong breeze swept in through the open window. It picked up the fairy dust and whipped it into a whirlwind of glitter. Then, the whirlwind lifted Kirsty gently into the air and carried her right out the window!

Trouble in Fairyland

Kirsty was whisked through the sky in a whirl of colorful fairy dust. She flew over rivers, mountains, trees, and houses, passing fluffy white clouds on the way. Soon, she saw the red-and-white toadstool houses of Fairyland below her. There was the river, winding its way

through the green hills. The water sparkled like diamonds in the golden sunshine.

The wind was bringing Kirsty down now, close to the silver Fairy Palace and its pretty pink towers. Kirsty could see King Oberon and Queen Titania waiting for her with a group of fairies. And next to the queen was someone else that Kirsty knew very well.

"Rachel!" called Kirsty.

Rachel rushed over as Kirsty landed gently on the grass. "I came the same way you did," Rachel explained excitedly, giving Kirsty a hug. "My snow globe broke, and the fairy dust brought me here."

"Do you know why?" asked Kirsty.

Rachel shook her head as the king and queen and their fairies joined the girls.

“It’s wonderful to see you both,” said Queen Titania, smiling. “But I’m afraid we need your help again,” she added, looking worried.

“I hope you don’t mind us bringing you here like this,” King Oberon said.

“Of course not!” Kirsty said eagerly. “Is something wrong?”

The queen sighed. “I’m afraid that Jack Frost is up to his old tricks again.”

Rachel looked shocked. “But he promised not to harm the Rainbow Fairies anymore!” she said, glancing up at the sky with a shiver. The sun had disappeared, and it had turned suddenly chilly.

“That’s true,” Queen Titania replied. “Unfortunately, he didn’t promise not to harm our Weather Fairies!” She waved

her hand at the seven fairies standing nearby.

"You mean this strange weather is all because of Jack Frost?" asked Kirsty, as sunshine broke through the gray clouds again.

The queen nodded. "Doodle, our weather vane rooster, is in charge of Fairyland's weather," she explained. "Doodle's tail is made up of seven

beautiful feathers. Each feather controls one kind of weather."

"Every morning, Doodle decides on the best weather for every part of Fairyland," the king went on. "Then he gives each Weather Fairy the correct feather, and they go off to do their weather work."

Rachel and Kirsty were listening hard.

"Come with us," said the queen. "We'll show you what's happened."

The king and queen led Rachel and Kirsty into the palace gardens and over to a golden pond.

The queen scattered some fairy dust onto the water, and it began to fizz and bubble.

After a moment, the water grew still and clear. A picture began to appear on the surface. It showed a beautiful rooster with a magnificent tail of red, gold, and copper-colored feathers.

"That's Doodle," the queen explained. "Yesterday morning he

planned the weather for Fairyland, like he always does."

Rachel and Kirsty watched as Doodle flew to the top of the palace and perched on one of the pink towers. He spun slowly around, gazing out over the hills of Fairyland. Then he nodded his feathery head and flew down again.

"Jack Frost has always helped Doodle and our Weather Fairies with the winter weather," the king continued. "There's so much work, with all the ice and snow and frost. But now it's summer, and Jack Frost has nothing to do."

"So he's bored," the queen put in. "And that means trouble! Look. . . ." She

pointed at the pictures appearing on the water.

Doodle was standing on the palace steps, waiting for the Weather Fairies to collect their feathers.

Kirsty gasped. "Look, Rachel!" she cried. "The goblins!"

Rachel remembered the goblins. They were Jack Frost's servants, and they were mean and selfish. They had big feet, pointed noses, and ugly faces.

Seven goblins were creeping toward Doodle. The rooster did not see them until it was too late. The goblins reached out and snatched Doodle's tail feathers. Then, they ran away with the feathers, laughing as they went.

"Oh no!" said Kirsty, as the rooster chased after the goblins. "Poor Doodle!"

"It gets worse." The queen sighed. "The goblins escaped into the human world, and Doodle followed them. And now Doodle is very far away from Fairyland, and without his magic tail feathers, his powers just won't work," she explained.

"Doodle turned into an ordinary metal weather vane," the king said sadly. "We don't even know where he is now."

"We need you to find the goblins," the queen said. "It's the only way to get Doodle's tail feathers back. Until then, Doodle is stuck in your world, and our weather will be all mixed up!" She looked up at the sky as a few raindrops began to fall. "The goblins are causing weather trouble for humans, too."

"Our Weather Fairies will help you," the king told the girls. "Let me introduce

you. This is Crystal the Snow Fairy, Abigail the Breeze Fairy, Pearl the Cloud Fairy, Goldie the Sunshine Fairy, Evie the Mist Fairy, Storm the Lightning Fairy, and Hayley the Rain Fairy."

The fairies gathered around Rachel and Kirsty. "Pleased to meet you!" they cried in sweet voices. "Thank you for helping us!"

"Each Weather Fairy will help you find her own feather," said the queen. "And we know the goblins are hiding somewhere here. . . ."

She sprinkled more fairy dust over the water, and the picture changed. Now, Rachel and Kirsty could see a pretty town surrounded by lush green fields.

"Oh!" Kirsty exclaimed. "That's Wetherbury! That's where I live. So *that's* why we had the snowstorm. It was the goblins!"

"What snowstorm?" asked Rachel.

Kirsty quickly explained. "And I think I know where Doodle is, too," she went on eagerly. "I think he's the rusty old weather vane my dad found in the park!"

"Thank goodness Doodle is safe!" cried Queen Titania happily.

"But the snowstorm means that one of the goblins is close to your town," the king warned. "And he must have Doodle's magic Snow Feather!"

Kirsty turned to Rachel. "Do you think your parents will let you come and stay

with me?" she said. "My mom said it was OK."

"I'll ask them," Rachel replied. "Then we can get the feathers back from the goblins!"

The king nodded. "That would be wonderful," he said.

The queen stepped forward. She had two golden lockets in her hand. "Each locket is filled with fairy dust," she explained, giving them to the girls. "You can use a pinch of this whenever you need to turn yourself into fairies and back

into humans again. But remember!" She smiled at Rachel and Kirsty. "Don't look too hard for magic — it will find you. And when it does, you will know that one of the magic feathers is close by."

The girls fastened the lockets around their necks.

"And beware of the goblins," the king added. "Jack Frost has cast a spell to make them bigger than usual."

"Bigger!" Rachel said, feeling nervous. "As big as humans, you mean?"

The king shook his head. "We have a law in Fairyland that not even magic can make anything bigger than the highest tower of the Fairy Palace." He pointed at the tallest pink tower. "But it means that now the goblins are almost as tall as your shoulders — when you're human-size."

Kirsty shivered. "We'll have to be careful," she said. "But of course we're happy to help."

Rachel nodded.

"Thank you," said the king gratefully. "We knew you wouldn't let us down."

The queen scattered fairy dust over the girls. It whipped around them, and in a few seconds, a whirlwind was gently lifting them up into the sky.

"Good-bye!" Kirsty and Rachel called,

waving at their friends below. "And don't worry. We'll find Doodle's feathers and bring him safely home."

"Rachel's here!" Kirsty shouted, rushing to the front door.

The Walkers' car was just turning in to the driveway.

"Put on your boots before you go out in the snow," called Mrs. Tate from the kitchen. Kirsty pulled on her boots. It was the day after she and Rachel had been to Fairyland, and Rachel's parents had agreed that she could come and stay with the Tates. Kirsty had been worried that the Walkers wouldn't be able to make it to Wetherbury, though. The goblins had been up to their tricks again.

There had been a heavy snowfall, and flakes were still drifting down.

Kirsty ran outside, followed by her mom and dad. The Walkers were unloading Rachel's suitcase from the car.

"Hello," called Mr. Tate. "Sorry about the weather. Isn't it awful?"

"I packed my boots, scarf, and gloves in my suitcase," Rachel whispered to Kirsty as they hugged hello.

"Would you like to come in for some coffee?" Mrs. Tate asked.

"That would be nice," Rachel's mom agreed. "But we shouldn't stay too long, in case the snow gets worse."

"Come and see Doodle," Kirsty said quietly to Rachel, as their parents chatted.

Mr. Tate had put Doodle inside the hall closet. Gently, Kirsty lifted the weather vane out.

"Oh, poor Doodle!" said Rachel when she saw the rusty rooster. "We have to find his feathers, Kirsty!"

A knock at the front door made them both turn.

"I wonder who that is?" Kirsty said, putting Doodle away again.

Kirsty's mom had opened the door and

was talking to an old lady who was bundled up in winter clothes.

"It's Mom's friend, Mrs. Fordham," Kirsty whispered to Rachel. "She lives on Willow Hill."

"I'm sorry to bother you," Mrs. Fordham was saying, "but there's so much snow, I can't get back to my house. I wondered if I could wait here for a while."

"Of course," said Mrs. Tate, helping her inside. "Come and have a cup of coffee."

"I've never seen weather like this," Mrs. Fordham went on, unwinding her scarf. "And it seems to be worse on Willow Hill than anywhere else. I don't know why."

Kirsty and Rachel glanced at each other.

"Why do you think there's more snow on Willow Hill?" Rachel whispered to Kirsty.

Kirsty looked excited. "Maybe that's where the goblin has taken the Snow Feather!"

"Let's go and find out," Rachel suggested.

Kirsty ran to ask her mom if she and Rachel could go out to play in the snow. Meanwhile, Rachel quickly changed out of her summer clothes. The girls said good-bye to their parents and hurried outside. It was still snowing.

"Quick," said Kirsty. "We have to make it to Willow Hill before the goblin gets away."

"Wait for me!" called a tiny voice behind them.

Kirsty and Rachel spun around.

A tiny fairy with crystal-colored wings was sliding down the gutter pipe. She wore a soft blue dress with fluffy white edging. Her wand was tipped with silver, and her hair was in pigtails.

"Look! It's Crystal the Snow Fairy!" Kirsty gasped.

The girls rushed over to her. "Hello again!" Crystal called. She looked excited. Tiny, sparkling snowflakes fizzed from the tip of her wand. "Look at all this snow," Rachel said.

"We think your feather is close by."

"So do I," agreed Crystal. "I can't wait to find it! But there must be a goblin nearby, too. . . ." She shivered, and her wings drooped. "We have to be careful."

"We're going to Willow Hill," Kirsty explained. "We think the feather may be over there."

Crystal fluttered down and landed on Rachel's shoulder. "Let's go!" she cried.

They headed out of the Tates' garden and walked up Twisty Lane onto High Street. There were lots of people around, so Crystal hid inside a fold of Rachel's scarf.

Crowds of children were playing in the park, throwing snowballs and building snowmen. They were having fun, but the snow was causing lots of problems, too. The girls passed a few cars that were stuck in snowdrifts. There were other cars that had broken down. A broken pipe at the post office had flooded the road, and some of the shops were closed.

"How much farther is Willow Hill?" Rachel panted. It was hard work, tramping through the deep snow.

Kirsty pointed up ahead of them. "There it is," she replied breathlessly.

Rachel's heart sank. The snow-covered hill looked very high. As they trudged out of the village, the snow seemed to be getting deeper, too. It was almost up to the top of Rachel's boots.

"I have an idea," Kirsty said suddenly, as her feet sank into a snowdrift. "Why don't we use some of our fairy dust? Then we can fly the rest of the way!"

Crystal popped her head out of Rachel's scarf. "Good idea!" she said.

Kirsty and Rachel opened their lockets. They each took a pinch of fairy dust and sprinkled it over themselves. Immediately, they began to shrink, and wings grew from their shoulders.

“Come on.” Crystal took their hands. “Let’s fly to the top of the hill. I can see a house up there.”

“That’s Willow Cottage,” explained Kirsty. “It’s Mrs. Fordham’s house.”

Crystal and the girls flew to the top of the hill, dodging the falling snowflakes, which seemed as big as dinner plates to Rachel and Kirsty.

As they got closer to the cottage, Kirsty spotted smoke coming from the chimney. “That’s funny!” she said with a frown. “Mrs. Fordham lives by herself,

and she's at our house. So who started the fire?"

"Let's look inside," suggested Crystal.

The three girls swooped down and hovered outside a frosty window. Crystal waved her wand to melt some of the frost, making a small peephole. They peered inside.

Sitting on the floor, in front of a roaring fire, was a big goblin. And in his hand was a shimmering copper feather, spotted with snowy-white dots.

Crystal gasped. "The Snow Feather!" she whispered excitedly.

A Sneaky Plan

As Kirsty, Rachel, and Crystal watched, the goblin sneezed loudly.

"A-CCCH-O-O-O!" When the goblin sneezed, a shower of ice cubes clattered to the floor. They began to melt, leaving behind little puddles of water.

"The goblin doesn't know how to use the magic feather properly," Crystal whispered.

Kirsty and Rachel were a little frightened. Because of Jack Frost's spell, the goblin was now pretty big. He looked very scary with his mean face, pointed ears, and big, flat feet.

The goblin huddled closer to the fire. He was grumbling and rubbing his toes. "I'm so cold," he moaned. "And my feet hurt!"

Crystal smiled. "Goblins hate to have cold feet!" she murmured.

"How are we going to get the feather back?" asked Kirsty.

"Let's fly around the house and look for a way in," Rachel suggested.

They flew around, checking all the windows and doors. But everything was locked. They could still hear the goblin muttering about his cold feet.

Kirsty grinned. "I have an idea!" she said. "Dad just decided to give away a pair of slippers that were too small for him. If I wrap them up in a box, I can deliver the package to the goblin.

Then he'll open the door for us, and we can get inside."

"Perfect!" Crystal agreed, as her wand fizzed sparkly snowflakes. "The goblin won't be able to resist a present. And if Rachel and I hide inside the box, maybe we can get the feather back."

Quickly, they all flew back to the Tates' house. With a wave of her wand, Crystal turned Kirsty human-size again. Then she and Rachel hid inside Kirsty's pockets.

Kirsty let herself quietly into the house and found the slippers, which her dad had put in a pile to give away. Then she wrapped the slippers in lots of tissue paper and put them in a shoe box.

"You can come out now," she whispered to Crystal and Rachel. Luckily, all the parents were chatting with Mrs. Fordham in the living room, and hadn't heard a thing.

Crystal and Rachel flew into

the shoe box and hid under the tissue paper.

Kirsty popped the lid back on the box and wrapped it neatly in brown paper. Then she set off again for Willow Hill. She couldn't fly up the hill with the package, so she had to walk.

By the time she reached Willow Cottage, Kirsty was out of breath and wet with snow. "We're here," she said quietly

to Crystal and Rachel. Then she took a deep breath, knocked on the door, and waited.

There was no reply. Kirsty knocked again. "Delivery!" she called.

"Go away!" the goblin shouted.

Kirsty tried again. "Some nice warm slippers for Mr. Goblin!" she said loudly.

This time the door opened, just a crack. Kirsty held the package out. The door opened wider, and a bony hand shot out and grabbed the box.

Then the door was slammed shut in Kirsty's face. Kirsty hurried to the window and peeked in. The goblin was tearing the paper off the shoe box. He pulled out the slippers, popped them on his feet, and stomped around the room to try them out.

They were a bit big, but he looked delighted. He settled down happily in a chair by the fire, stretched out his feet to

admire the slippers, and fell fast asleep. The shining Snow Feather lay on his lap.

Kirsty watched as the tissue paper in the box began to move. Crystal and Rachel fluttered out.

Crystal flew over to the snoring goblin and lifted the feather from his lap.

“You’d better make me human-size again, Crystal,” Rachel whispered. “Then I can open the window and we can escape.”

Crystal nodded. She waved her wand over Rachel, who instantly shot up to

her full size. Then Rachel unlatched the window and pushed it open.

An icy blast of wind swept into the room.

"What's going on?" the goblin roared, jumping up from his armchair.

A Very Unusual Snowball

"Quick!" Kirsty gasped, pulling Rachel through the window.

Crystal flew out too, her face pale with fear.

The goblin spotted the Snow Fairy and gave another furious roar. He ran over to the window, jumped out, and followed the girls.

Kirsty and Rachel hurried down the hill. It was hard to run fast because the snow was so deep.

"Hurry!" Crystal called. She was flying above them, the feather in her hand. "He's getting closer!"

Rachel glanced anxiously over her shoulder. The goblin was catching up!

But then she saw him fall over in his too-big slippers. Yelling loudly, he rolled head over heels down the hill, picking up snow as he went.

"Watch out, Kirsty!" Rachel gasped. "The goblin's turned into a giant snowball!"

The goblin's arms and legs stuck out of the snowball as it rolled down the hill. Quickly, the girls dove out of the way. The snowball shot past them and rolled away, faster and faster. Soon it was out of sight.

"Are you all right?" asked Crystal, flying over to her friends.

The girls were picking themselves up and brushing snow from their clothes.

"We're fine!" Kirsty beamed. "But can you stop the Snow Feather's magic?"

Crystal nodded and expertly waved the Snow Feather in a complicated pattern. Immediately, the snow clouds vanished. Overhead, the sky was blue and the sun shone.

By the time the girls made their way back to the Tates' house, the snow had melted away.

As Kirsty and Rachel walked into the house, with Crystal safely hidden in Kirsty's pocket, Mrs. Tate smiled.

"Hello, girls," she said. "Isn't it funny how the weather's changed? Your mom and dad have gone home, Rachel. At least they won't have to worry about the snow now. I hope it stays nice for the rest of your visit."

Kirsty and Rachel grinned at each other.

"Your dad's in the garden, Kirsty," Mrs. Tate went on. "He's attaching that old weather vane to the barn roof."

Kirsty and Rachel ran outside. They looked up on top of the barn — and there was Doodle! Mr. Tate was busy in his shed, so he wasn't watching.

"Quick, Crystal." Kirsty took the Snow Fairy out of her pocket. "Give Doodle his tail feather back!"

Crystal nodded. Fluttering her shiny wings, she flew up to Doodle and put the big tail feather into place.

The girls gasped in surprise as copper and gold sparkles fizzed and flew from Doodle's tail. The iron weather vane vanished. In its place was Doodle, just as colorful as he had been in Fairyland!

Doodle turned his head and stared straight at Kirsty and Rachel. "Beware!" he squawked. But before he could say

any more, his feathers began to stiffen and he became metal again.

"What was he trying to say?" Rachel asked, puzzled.

Kirsty shook her head. She had no idea.

"I don't know either," sighed Crystal.

"But it must be important. What if he was trying to warn us about other goblins?"

Kirsty frowned. "Maybe he'll be able to tell us more when we bring back his other feathers."

"Yes," Crystal agreed. She waved at Rachel and Kirsty. "And now that you've found the Snow Feather, I have to return to Fairyland. The king and queen will be so happy. Good-bye, and thank you!"

"Good-bye!" Rachel and Kirsty called.

The girls waved as Crystal flew up into the sky, her wings glittering in the sun.

Kirsty turned to Rachel. "And now we have only six more magic feathers to find," she said.

Rachel nodded. "I wonder where the next one will be!"

Rachel and Kirsty looked at the sunny sky and wondered what adventure — and weather — the next week would bring.

RAINBOW magic™

THE WEATHER FAIRIES

Crystal found her weather feather,
and it stopped snowing in summer.
Now Rachel and Kirsty must help

Join them for a windy adventure!

RAINBOW magic™ SPECIAL EDITION

Three Books in Each One— More Rainbow Magic Fun!

Joy the Summer Vacation Fairy
Holly the Christmas Fairy
Kylie the Carnival Fairy
Stella the Star Fairy
Shannon the Ocean Fairy
Trixie the Halloween Fairy
Gabriella the Snow Kingdom Fairy
Juliet the Valentine Fairy
Mia the Bridesmaid Fairy
Flora the Dress-Up Fairy
Paige the Christmas Play Fairy
Emma the Easter Fairy
Cara the Camp Fairy
Destiny the Rock Star Fairy
Belle the Birthday Fairy
Olympia the Games Fairy
Selena the Sleepover Fairy
Cheryl the Christmas Tree Fairy
Florence the Friendship Fairy

SCHOLASTIC
scholastic.com
rainbowmagiconline.com

RMSPECIAL10